Beauty
AND THE
Beast

A PARRAGON BOOK

Published by
Parragon Books,
Unit 13-17, Avonbridge Trading Estate,
Atlantic Road, Avonmouth, Bristol BS11 9QD

Produced by
The Templar Company plc,
Pippbrook Mill, London Road, Dorking, Surrey RH4 1JE

Designed by Mark Kingsley-Monks

Printed and bound in Italy

ISBN 0-75250-949-7

Beauty
— AND THE —
Beast

Retold by Stephanie Laslett
Illustrated by Alison Winfield

There was once a wealthy merchant, who had three daughters. One day, as he prepared to leave on a long journey, he asked each of them what gifts they would like from the lands across the sea.

One daughter longed for a mirror and one wished for a fine crown sparkling with jewels, but his youngest and favourite daughter asked only for a perfect red rose.

So the merchant sailed away and once his business was done he began to search for his daughter's gifts. He found a beautiful mirror and a richly jewelled crown soon enough but although he hunted high and low in the gardens of kings and the bowers of emperors still he could not fine a perfect red rose.

He could not bear to return home without a present for his precious girl and so he sailed ever on in search of the rose. One day a pirate ship drew alongside and the merchant was robbed of all he possessed. Laughing cruelly, the pirates tossed him overboard and sailed off into the distance.

The merchant swam for his life and at last reached the shore of a strange land. Thick forest stretched as far as the eye could see and so the poor man set off to look for signs of life. Silence hung about him; no birds sang, no creatures stirred. After a time he came upon a path and to his great amazement it led him to a palace.

It sparkled in the sunlight as if cut from the purest crystal and as the merchant explored each room sweet music filled the air. "This is a palace fit for a king," he thought to himself, "but why is it completely deserted?"

Outside in the magnificent garden the merchant strolled amongst the flowers. Suddenly he stopped in amazement, for there in the middle of a little clearing was a rose bush covered with perfect roses. But as he knelt and picked one beautiful bloom, a terrible roar filled the air.

The poor merchant cowered in terror as a hideous Beast appeared.

"Forgive me for taking your flower!" he begged. "It was a gift for my youngest daughter, who would have loved it dearly." The Beast frowned.

"Then she must take your place and stay here," he said. "If she comes of her own free will I will spare your life." With that he gave the man a gold ring. "Put this ring on her finger and send her to me within three days or you shall die!" As he took the ring, the man found himself back outside his own home!

When he told his strange story to his youngest daughter she threw her arms around his neck. "I will go gladly, father," she cried. "The Beast will surely not keep me there forever."

And so on the third day she slipped the ring on her finger and her father bade her farewell with a heavy heart.

In an instant the young girl found herself in a beautiful garden, close by a rose bush and the rose that her father had picked for her lifted from her hand and was bound once again to its stem where it bloomed even brighter than before.

Slowly she explored the palace room by room, marvelling at the many fine treasures to be seen at every turn. When she grew hungry she found a table laid with finest crystal and china and suddenly good food appeared upon her plate.

As she sat at the table the girl was astonished to see a strange message appear upon the wall.

"Welcome, pure Beauty,
and have no fear
For you are truly Mistress here."

Then the words disappeared and the great palace was silent. Who could it have been?

Beauty felt no fear and begged aloud to meet the kind person who was taking such good care of her. Reluctantly he agreed and at first his snarling roar filled her with terror, but he spoke words of such gentle kindness that she soon forgot her fear. From then on Beauty and the Beast spoke each day.

As time passed Beauty longed not just to hear but also to see her master.

"I am afraid to do as you ask," replied the Beast sadly, "for I am sure you will be filled with loathing at the sight of me and that I could not bear." But Beauty pleaded and begged until at last he agreed to grant her wish.

"Come to the garden at dusk and then we will meet," he said. And so, as the lengthening shadows spread across the ground, he stood before her. But the sight so frightened her that, just as he had feared, she fell quite senseless to the ground.

Soon Beauty had recovered and as she sat up she could see the poor Beast sobbing bitterly. All fear left her and she felt nothing but pity and sorrow. So she rested her hand upon his shoulder and raised his great face to look at her own.

"Do not cry," she whispered. "I do not fear your form. It is only a shell which cloaks a tender heart. The wisdom that lies within is good and true. Please forgive me for hurting you so." The Beast's terrible face creased in a smile and from that day on they became loving friends — the ugly Beast and the delicate Beauty.

But after a time Beauty longed to see her dear father once again and so asked the Beast if she might return home. His face became sorrowful.

"You may leave here for three days only and then you must return," he said. "I love you so much that I could not live without you." Beauty looked up at him tenderly and agreed to do as he asked. She slipped the golden ring upon her finger once again and in a flash found herself back in her own garden. Her father was overjoyed to hear that she was happy but her two sisters felt nothing but revulsion for the horrible Beast.

"He may appear hideous," replied Beauty, "but underneath he is the kindest and most gentle of beings." But the two sisters were jealous of her happiness and as the last hour of the third day ticked away, they turned back the hands of the clock.

So it was that Beauty returned late to the palace and broke the Beast's heart. She found him lying dead in the garden clutching a single red rose to his breast.

Slowly she bent to kiss his cheek and a single tear fell from her eye and landed on his heart.

All at once Beauty found herself in a great hall surrounded by noblemen and ladies, and holding the hand of a handsome Prince.

"Dear Beauty," he said tenderly. "Long ago I was cursed by an evil witch and she turned me into a dreadful Beast. But for your love I would have remained so. You saw beneath the ugliness and broke the spell and you alone have set me free. I have come to love you truly and now ask that you be my queen, and stay with me forever." And so it was that the Beauty married her Beast and they both lived happily ever more.

Madame de Villeneuve

The *Beauty and the Beast* was first written
by Madame de Villeneuve and
published in 1740.
A far simpler version of the story was written by
Madame de Beaumont in 1756 and translated
into English the following year.
The basic theme of the story spoken youth and
maid in many other worlds over the ...
two generous souls who live in mutual accord
within ... through the strength of their love,
is transferred into a human.
Madame de Beaumont ... a moral power ...
... admirable element. She wrote it while
working as a governess in England and evidently
believed that the story's moral message added to
its important lesson for her young charges.